Unforgettable Love

Unforgettable Love

Patricia Lee

Printed in the United States of America

Publishing services by Selah Publishing Group, Bristol, Tennessee. The views expressed or implied in this work do not necessarily reflect those of Selah Publishing Group.

ISBN: 978-1-58930-316-4
Library of Congress Control Number: 2020908869

Dedication

This book is dedicated,
with love,
to my family,
along with Chase and Kier for all their help

Acknowledgments

This story is what it is because of all the people that have touched my life. I have always had such a special place in my heart for the gypsy people. So, creating Helena was so much fun.

Contents

Chapter One

❧

ELENA'S EYES OPEN UP AS SHE HEARD THE LANDING GEAR COMING out. She looked over to see Steve straightening up in his seat. "You better put your seat up we are going to land in a few minutes", Steve told his wife. "We are here already?", Helena asked him. "Look out your window the small piece of land is your new home for 24 months. That is the island of Guam", he explained to her. "It is so small", Helena said looking out her window. "Yes, it is. There are three military bases there plus the local people", he explained. "The ocean is so beautiful. I hope we won't live to far from the beach", Helena noticed. "There is a beach on the base. I just hope our housing is ready", Steve told her. "Me too", Helena agreed.

Helena waited quietly while Steve got their paperwork ready so they could get checked into the base. Helena was so happy to have a new life with Steve away from the craziness off her gypsy family. Molly was so right. She does have a lot of living ahead of her with a wonderful husband.

There was a bus waiting for them as they got off the airplane. It would take them to the air force base. "This is the smallest airport I have ever seen!", Helena exclaimed. As they were getting on the bus, Helena noticed another couple. "I wonder if they are going to the base", she said to Steve. Helena spoke to the girl. She had not seen them on the plane. The rest of the people stayed on as they were going on to the Philippines and Vietnam. "Hi, are you going to Anderson AFB?", Helena asked. "Yes, we are", the woman responded. "So, are we! Where do you come from?", Helena continued. "Westover AFB in Massachusetts", the woman said. "Us too", Helena told her. Steve turned around and put out his hand, "I am Steve Cliff, and this is my wife Helena". " Hi, I am Mike Taylor, and this is my wife Ginger", the man responded. "What did you do at Westover Mike?", Steve asked. "I am a fire fighter. I was just re-up'd again for four more. I liked my job and Ginger likes to travel so we are excited about being on Guam. We hope to do some R&R to Europe and Hong Kong while we are stationed here", Mike said.

The bus pulled into the check-in station. Steve got their bags and things and went in the building. "Hope to see you two on base. Let's get together when we both get settled in", Mike said. "I will look you up Mike", Steve responded. "Sounds Good", Mike agreed. "They seem like a nice couple. It will be nice to know someone here", Helena told her husband as they walked away.

Steve got all the paperwork taken care of and their new ID cards. "What do we have to do now Steve? I am getting hungry", Helena asked. "Me Too. We are done with all this red tape. Let's go and get something to eat then we can go see our new house", Steve told her. "It's ready?", she asked excitedly. "Yes, I got the keys and the address", he told her. They walked down the street to a little hamburger place. They ordered their food and found a table outside. "It seems strange to me everything is outside, even the movie theatre", Helena noticed. "It's an island, Helena, in the middle of the Pacific Ocean. It's very warm here all the time", Steve explained. "That's fine with me. I was sick of that cold winter in Massachusetts", Helena said. "Well, you won't be seeing any cold weather for a long time. Maybe rain during the rainy season", he told her.

"Let's finish eating and go see our new house", Helena was excited to see their new place. "Okay, I've got to call my sponsor to come pick us up. There's a pay phone over there", Steve walked over to the phone and made the call.

Helena couldn't help but think how wonderful this was. A new place to live. A great husband. A new adventure in life. Molly was so right. I do have so much living to do. Steve said to her, "Come on grab your suitcase here comes our ride". "Steve, I was just thinking about Molly, do you think I will ever see her again?", Helena asked. "Yes", Steve laughed "in about three to six months Gary's squadron will be shipped out". "Really?", Helena asked. "Yes. Gary wouldn't like it, but it is sure to happen", Steve told her. "Oh, I hope it does", Helena said. She really misses her best friend Molly and they have just arrived in Guam.

As they were getting into the car, the man said, "Hi I am Sergeant Green. I'm here to get you settled in". "Great", Steve put out his hand, "I am Sergeant Steve Cliff. This is my wife Helena". Helena responded, "I am so excited to see where we will live". Sargent Green told them it would not take long they were just a few blocks away. "Everything is pretty close here. This housing area is for the enlisted guys", Sargent Green explained. "Not too bad", Steve responded. "They are small but still plenty of room. I have lived in a lot worse", he told them, "I live on the street behind you".

"Here it is, your new home", Sergeant Green told them as they pulled into the drive. "They all look the same. Concrete with stucco over it. Nice big screened-in porch", Helena observed. "Yes, that's called the lanai. You'll love it when it's not 95 degrees", Sergeant Green explained. "At least there is always an island breeze", Helena noted. As they unlocked the door and went in, Helena said, "I love it" and started looking around. "It has two bedrooms. There is a bed in here", she said. "Yes, they give you a bed and couple chairs". Sergeant Green asked Steve, "When do you expect your household things to arrive?". "I am hoping this week", Steve responded. "My wife sent over a set of sheets and some towels to hold you over. At least you can make your bed and take a shower", Sergeant Green said. "Thank you so much. That will help. If our things don't come soon, we can always go to the Px and get a few things", Steve responded. "Sergeant Green would you mind taking us over to the commissaire to get a few groceries?" He agreed to do so. Helena was checking out the kitchen. "Come on Helena!", Steve called for his wife. As they were driving over to the commissaire, Steve said, "Sergeant Green, I will need a car. If you hear of any old ones at a good price will you let me know?". "I sure will. There are always cars here to buy when the guys come in. The enlisted guys can't afford to ship cars home, so they use them for a couple years then sell them when they ship out. I will keep my eyes open. I am sure I can find you something to drive", Sergeant Green explained.

Helena got what they needed to get them started. All the staples to fix a meal without a lot of pots or pans. Hopefully, their things would come pretty soon. Helena got checked out and said "Let's get back to our house Steve. I think we are all done here Sergeant Green". "Alright, I know you must be ready to settle in for the evening. Do you have to report to work in the morning Steve?" "Yes, I do", Steve responded. "How are you getting there?", Sergeant Green asked. "They are sending someone to pick me up", Steve told him. As he let them out on the driveway, he told them to let him know if they needed anything. Steve and Helena thanked him.

Steve carried in the groceries and put them down on the counter. "I am going in to put the sheets on the bed. You want to help?", Helena asked. Steve looked at Helena. "You want to try out the new bed?", he asked. Helena smiled and giggled as she ran back to the bedroom. Steve grabbed Helena and kissed her. She kissed him back. "I love you Steve. Never let me go".

He started to lay her down on the bed and she stopped him. "Wait at least let me make the bed", she said. "Oh, okay I guess that would be better. Then we will finish what we have started", he told her. Helena finished making the bed. "We don't have any pillows", she said. "That's okay Helena. We don't need any tonight. And, this sheet is all we need. It is so warm here in Guam", he assured her.

The morning came around fast and Helena woke up to see Steve dressed and ready to go to work. "Why didn't you wake me? I could have made you some coffee", she asked him. "You were sleeping so well I didn't want to wake you. I know you were tired from the long trip. And, then, last night", he told her. Helena looked at Steve and just smiled. There was a knock on the door. "That must be my ride. I will see you this evening", Steve said. Steve kissed Helena bye and walked to the door. Steve opened the door to see a tall red headed guy standing there. "Hi Sergeant Cliff, I am Airman Rick Steward". They shook hands. "Nice to meet you", Steve told the man. "I am here to take you to work. I hear you are from Westover AFB", the man said. "Yes", Steve responded. "Well, you have gone from cold weather to hot. It sure gets hot on the flight line. But you will get used to it. The base is really nice", he told Steve. "Yes, it is", Steve agreed. "This island is pretty but small. There are three military bases here. I have been here two years. I will be shipping out soon. I hear there are a lot of guys from Westover coming here. We need a lot of jet mechanics for all the planes mostly for the B52 Bomber. They are working over-time. Here's' our squadron", Rick continued, "Let's go in the hanger and let you meet everyone". Steve walked into a group of guys talking. He stopped and looked around. He heard someone say, "Welcome Sergeant Cliff to the 36 Air Wing. This is your maintenance area. I am Master Sergeant Cullen". "Very nice to meet you", Steve responded. "Let's go get you settled in", Sergeant Cullen said.

A few weeks had passed, and Helena had gotten the house in order. Everything had arrived safe and nothing broken. Steve liked his job. Helena loved the warm weather. She had not gotten any mail yet. Helena was hoping she would hear from Molly, she really misses her. She liked her neighbor. It was great meeting all the people in the neighborhood. Everyone was from someplace different and she loved not being judged because of it. The girl across the street was from Japan. She met her husband when he was stationed there. She was very nice, and Helena enjoyed her company although, she couldn't always understand what she was saying. The couple living right next door were from Tennessee. She was down to earth and was very much a sweetheart. She talked like Molly with that southern accent, but a lot more southern.

Helena was going to go out on the lanai when she saw the mailman coming down the street. She walked out to meet him. "I hope you have something for me!" she asked him excitedly. She was thrilled when he said back "I sure do, a couple letters from home it looks like". She thanked him and hurried off with the letters.

Helena looked to see who they were from. One from Molly and the other her Grandmother. She went into the house and opened the letters.

> *Dear Helena,*
> *Hope this finds you and Steve well. I guess by now you are all settled in. How do you like living on the air force base? I hear it is hot there. Well, I guess I will find out soon how hot it gets. I am so excited to tell you Gary got orders. We will be coming to Guam.*

Helena was so excited to read the good news. Molly and I will be together again. Helena read some more.

> *I guess you know Gary is not too happy. He really wanted to stay at Westover, but he could have got-*

ten orders for Vietnam, so we are happy that didn't happen. We should be there in about a month. We will make a fast trip to Indiana to see our family. Then, we will be headed that way. I hear it is a long trip. We will be shipping our things in about ten days. I look so forward to seeing you. I have so much to tell you. Take care.

Molly

Helena was so giddy to tell Steve that Molly and Gary were coming to Guam that she almost forgot about her grandmother's letter. As she was opening her grandmother's letter, she felt sad for a moment. She thought to herself, I really do miss her.

Dear Helena,
Hope you are well and happy in your new life. I miss seeing you. I am fine. Staying busy. There is always a new group of air force boys coming to get their palms read. Your mother is still missing her friend. She did get a post card from him. Haven't seen your father for several months. Please write me and let me know how you are. Thinking of you always.

Grandmother

Helena held the letter in her hands for a few minutes remembering how good her grandmother had always been to her. She was more like a mother to her.

Helena was so excited to think Molly would be there in a month. Steve was so right. I know he will be happy to see them.

Chapter Two

❦

THERE WAS A KNOCK ON THE DOOR. IT STARTLED HELENA FOR A moment. Who could that be? She went to the door and there stood Ginger Taylor, the girl she met at the airport that was on the plane with them.

"Hi Helena, remember me, I am Ginger" the woman said to her. "Sure, come on in" Helena said. "It is so nice to see a familiar face. How did you find me?". Ginger responded "We just live a couple blocks away and Mike got your address for me. I thought you might be a little homesick". "I sure have been". Helena said. The ladies continued talking and Ginger invited Helena to go to the base library to get some books to read. The two grabbed their purses and Helena locked the house up. Helena noticed Ginger's car and asked, "When did you get your car?". Ginger told her they got the car a couple weeks ago. Ginger explained to Helena, "I have been taking Mike to work so I could get out and do some things". Helena can't wait to get a car of their own and told Ginger that Steve is supposed to look at one after work tonight. She said "I hope it is a good one. We need some wheels of our own. We haven't even gotten to go to the beach or anything yet." Ginger told Helena how beautiful the beach was and how much she loved it there but warned her that the guys at the beach are all big flirts. She told Helena "They love looking at the girls in swimsuits. Mike won't let me go by myself or with a girlfriend. He is the jealous type." Helena was a little taken back but said "Well, I don't have to worry about that. I have never owned a swimsuit". "What?" Ginger questioned "With that figure what's wrong with you?!". "My family would not let me. But I'm sure Steve would. He is a wonderful guy", Helena explained.

Helena and Ginger arrived at the base library. "The base library is very nice, I am so glad we came", Helena told Ginger. "Yes, it is a great way to spend some time. I have never had much time to read, but I love to". Ginger announced to Helena, "I am going over here in the romance section. If you get your books before me, come get me". Helena told Ginger that she would get hers before her. After browsing some of the book selection Helena said to Ginger "You are a romantic I can tell". Ginger agreed back and said, "Yes, I am. I get lost in those books with all that mushy stuff". The romantic books reminded Helena once again of her dear friend Molly. Helena began to tell Ginger about her. "You will really like my friend Molly who will be here next month. Her husband is getting stationed here. Although, he sure didn't want to come to Guam. But Molly is my dearest friend. She is the reason I am married to Steve. She fixed us up and she helped me change my life". "What do you mean changed your life?" Ginger asked. Helena began to explain, "I was in love with someone and something happened to make it all go south. I didn't think I had much to live for. I will tell you about it sometime, but not today. That is the past and I want to stay in the now". Ginger understood and did not want to pry. Helena continued on about Molly, "You will really like Molly. I hope we can all be friends, she is such a fun and crazy girl" Ginger responded "I am sure we can all get along if you like her, she has to be a nice girl!". Helena laughed thinking about her crazy friend and said, "I hope Guam can handle her!". They both laughed together and got their books and headed out the door.

Ginger dropped Helena off at her house and wished her luck with the car shopping tonight. Helena thanked her and then Ginger pulled out of the driveway and headed back to her home.

As Helena was going in the house, she had a flash back of the day she was told that Andre had hung himself. She had not thought of him in a long time. Maybe if she had not loved him so much, he would not have had done that. They had such plans, but his family was not going to let him have a life with her all because she was from a family of gypsies and he was French. Her skin was a little darker than his. She was not good enough for them. She still, every once in a while, felt like he wasn't dead. She never got to see him. Everything was private. She never got to say her goodbye. She heard the door open and that made her jump. She heard Steve yell, "Anybody home?". A smiled washed across her face as she responded, "Yes, I am here. So glad to see you. How was your day?". Steve sat down next to her and said "It was fine. Met the guys on my crew. They all seem to be very nice". Helena remembered her own day and began to tell Steve, "Got a letter from Molly today. You were right, they will be here in about a month. She said Gary was not too happy". Steve was not surprised at the news but was excited for his wife to have her friend nearby again. He told her "He will like it when he gets here. The work is good, and we will be busy keeping the B52s in the air".

Helena began to tell Steve more about her day, "Ginger came by today and we went to the library. Got some good books to read, romance novels". Steve was not the least bit surprised at this news either, "I bet" he said and just looked at her and smiled. Helena told him how Ginger had Mike's car and how it was pretty nice for an old car. That brought to his attention the next thing on his to-do list for the day and Steve told Helena, "That reminds me, Sergeant Green is coming by to pick me up so I can go see this car he found for us. I hope it runs ok. We need something now". Helena told Steve she would fix dinner while he is gone and when he got back, they could have dinner out on the lanai. He told her it sounded great and asked what they were having. Helena told him, "Tuna fish sandwich and pork in beans and Kool-Aid." Steve said, "That's good enough for me" and went back to the bedroom to change out of his uniform into some jeans. Sergeant Green would be there soon.

It wasn't long and the doorbell rang. "What's that", Helena asked. "I bet that's the doorbell" Steve told her. They went to the door and there stood Sergeant Green. They told him to come on in and he stepped in the lanai. He asked Steve if he was ready to go and apologized for being late. Sergeant Green asked "How are you doing Helena? What do you think of this place?". She responded, "Oh, I like it and I just got word my best friend and her husband are being sent over here so I am thrilled about that!". Sergeant Green said back, "That's great! I bet he is coming from Westover AFB. Heard we are getting a squadron of jet mechanics. I was at Westover before we came over here. Really liked it. Let's get going and see if we can get you a car Steve". The two headed out the door.

Chapter Three

&

A few weeks had passed. Steve and Helena were settled in. Helena and Ginger had planned a day at the beach. Helena was very excited and nervous. She had bought a swimsuit at the base exchange. She had never had one and felt very uncomfortable, but she had tried it on for Steve and he told her how nice she looked in it. She didn't fell feel very nice but was going to give it a shot. Steve told her to go and have fun but to be careful not to get sun burned.

When they got to the beach, Helena couldn't get over how beautiful and white the sad was. Ginger said, "Let's put the blanket down over here. This looks like a good spot". Helena agreed and asked, "Have you seen anything like this?". Ginger responded, "No, it is beautiful. The water was so clear and blue. Look, there are some people surfing!". "I am going to learn how to do that while I am on this island", Ginger declared, "You want to take lessons with me Helena?". "Oh, no, not me. I will keep my feet on dry land but wait till my friend Molly gets here. She will want to take lessons. She will try anything", Helena told Ginger. "When will they be here?", Ginger asked. Helena told her that they should arrive by the end of next week.

Ginger grabbed Helena's hand and said, "Let's go put our feet in the ocean". Helena reluctantly agreed but told Ginger she was not getting in if it was cold. Ginger laughed and said, "Oh, it is cold only for a few minutes. You will get used to it". The waves were splashing up against Helena's legs. This is fun, she thought to herself. About that time another wave came in and knocked Helena down. She jumped up with a mouth full of saltwater. Ginger was laughing at her. She was frazzled and was not expecting it. Through her laughing Ginger asked Molly if she was okay. She responded, "Yes, but I am ready to go to the blanket. I never dreamed I'd be at a beach in the middle of the Pacific Ocean. And, of all things, in a swimsuit". Ginger couldn't stop laughing at her. Helena continued talking, "I went to the beach one time back in Massachusetts with Molly and Gary when Steve and I first met. But it was nothing like this. It had big rocks and the sand was brown and I sure didn't have on a swimsuit. It was summer, but it was cool. It never got real hot in Massachusetts. This is so much fun, but I think I will stay on top of the water". Ginger agreed that was a good idea.

"Ginger let's stay about an hour then we better get home. I don't want to get sun burned my first day at the beach", Helena explained. Ginger was teasing Helena about the guys that were checking her out in her swimsuit. Helena's face turned so red. She was embarrassed, "Stop that Ginger! They are not looking at me. It is you that has the figure!". Ginger laughed and responded, "Well I do look pretty good If I say so myself". Helena started laughing. Helena thought about Molly again, "Wow, you and Molly are going to hit it off great" she said. "I am looking forward to meeting this wonderful Molly you keep talking about" Ginger answered.

The time had come for Gary and Molly to arrive. Steve had made arrangements to pick them up at the airport. There was no housing available for them right now, but there were some apartments off base that they could rent. Steve had found one for them. Not as nice as the base, but it would do. All military people live there. It would be a few days before they could move in so Gary and Molly would be staying with them.

Helena told Steve, "Come on let's get going. Their plane might come in early". "Calm down Helena. We have plenty of time" he teased. "I am just so excited Steve. My wish has come true. I didn't think I would ever see Molly again and here we are going to be together again. I am just so happy. Could life get any better?" Helena exclaimed. She was over the moon her friend was finally arriving.

Well as usual, the plane was a little late. But Steve saw a plane coming in. He showed Helena where the plane was coming in. Helena started pacing back and forth and told her husband how excited she was again. He was happy too and told her it wouldn't be long now. Helena went over and stood by the gate. About twenty minutes had passed and people had started coming through the gate, but she didn't see Molly or Gary. She looked over at Steve. Where are they? Then she heard a voice yell, "Helena!", and Molly came running out the gate. They were both making so much noise everyone was looking their way. Gary walked right past them as they were hugging and talking a mile a minute. Steve put out his hand. "So glad to see you Gary. How was your flight?" he asked. Gary responded and said, "It was so long, but this is a small island". Steve told Gary he thought he would like it here. "I sure hope so. Two years is a long time", Gary responded as the two walked back over to the ladies.

"You think those two will calm down soon?", Steve asked, "Come on girls let's get the baggage and get going to the house. You two have plenty of time to talk". Molly said hi to Steve and gave him a hug. I am glad to be here she told him. "Not near as glad as Helena is that you are here" he told her. Helena gave Gary a quick little hug and told him she was glad to have him there. He said it was good to see her, too.

It didn't take long to get their baggage. Helena and Molly headed to the car. Molly and Helena had not taken a breath; it was nonstop talking. Steve looked over at Gary and just smiled and said, "I think they are happy to be together again". Steve told Gary, "You will like it here. It is busy on the flight line, but a lot of great guys. It does stay hot all the time. But you will get used to it". As they drove up to the base gate, the airman waved them through. Helena told Molly they would be at the house soon. "The base is real pretty with lots of palm trees", Molly said. "Yes, lots of white sand and coconut trees too. The military calls it the rock. The longer you are here the smaller it gets", Helena responded. "After you two get rested up from the long trip, we will give you the tour", Steve announced. Gary told Steve, "I have to report to my squadron in the morning and turn in my papers".

Morning came fast. Molly and Helena talked almost all night. Steve woke Gary up and said, "I will take you to report in for work. We will let the girls sleep. At least they are not talking right now", and they laughed. "We can grab a coffee at your squadron" Steve said. Gary agreed. Steve left a note telling Helena they would be back later.

A few weeks had passed. Molly and Helena had gotten caught up on a lot of their talking. Molly told Helena she has some news about her mother's friend back at Westover AFB. Molly wanted to pick the right time to tell her about the airman that her mother liked. But she knew she needed plenty of time to tell her everything. It was still so hard for Molly to wrap her head around the fact that she had seen and talked to her real father and never knew it. Even though she felt something when she bumped into him in the Px he must have felt something too because he turned around and watched her for a minute. Helena's Grandmother was so right. He was closer than she knew. It made her sad to think he never knew that girl he bumped into was his own daughter. But some things just don't always work out the way you want.

Molly heard someone yell, "Are you home?". She went to the front door and there stood Helena. "What are you doing?" Helena asked. "Not much. Mostly daydreaming", Molly told her. "What are you doing here in the middle of the day?", she asked. Helena told her how Steve had picked up their car a couple days ago she had taken him to work so she could go see her. "I was curious about what you said the other day about my Mother's friend" she told her. "Let's' go sit down. I have some sun tea made. It doesn't take it long to brew when you put it in the hot Guam sun", Molly said.

They went out and sat on the lanai. "I just love these porches or lanai. I have never heard a porch called a lanai, but I have never been to Guam either" Molly said. "So, come on Molly, tell me what you know", Helena insisted. "Well, you know I went to Kentucky to find out about my real father when we were on leave before we went home to Indiana? "Yes, I knew that", Helena responded. "Well, I found my real father's grave" Molly said. "Oh, that's wonderful Molly" Helena responded. "Yes, it was a good thing and I met my Grandmother. She was very happy to meet me. She said she knew I would come". "Why did she say that?". "Well, it turns out that my real father had just died a couple months before I got there, and the strange thing was that he had been at Westover AFB. He had been in the air force for over twenty years and I had bumped into him when I was in the Px" she explained. Helena could not believe what she was hearing. "My grandmother showed me a picture of him. I could not believe my eyes. I still can't", Molly said. Molly started to cry, "Your grandmother was so right Helena. She told me my father was closer than you think". "Don't cry Molly. It just wasn't meant to be. At least you got to see what he looked like". "Yes, I did. But, Molly, what does this have to do with me?", Helena questioned.

"Well, the thing is that the airman that your mother was so crazy about was my real father". Helena just looked at Molly with disbelief. "No way!" she said. "Yes, I saw him at your house many times. And, he is dead". "Yes, remember your mother said she was going to a hospital in Texas before he got discharged". "Yes, that is right". "Oh, my mother is going to be so sad. You know Molly, he was really a nice guy. I talked to him a few times. But he always seemed sad to me. I guess, now I know why".

Chapter Four

ANOTHER MONTH HAD ROLLED AROUND, AND MOLLY AND GARY were in the base housing and settled in. Helena and Steve lived within walking distance. And, Mike and Ginger were a few blocks away. They all had become good friends.

Molly and Helena were spending a lot of time together. They had gotten into a card club with some of the girls on base. Ginger was always taking Molly and Helena on some adventure. She was always looking for new things to do. Molly liked her so much. Helena liked her too but thought she was a little crazy in a good way.

Molly, Helena, and Ginger had gone off base to what they called the town of Guam. There were few stores and a lot of just small shops with all kinds of local stuff in them. Molly wanted to find a few things to send home to her sisters. There was some beautiful jewelry made out of the coral that was on the island. Helena was looking at a necklace that had some beautiful blue stones in it. Molly walked up to her and said "Buy it. You would look good with that around your neck". Helena laughed. "You know me better than that. I wouldn't wear that. You are the girl with the beads and bangles. You would think you were the gypsy instead of me". Molly just laughed. "You got a point there Helena. I do love all that stuff and the lipstick and to smell good".

"I was thinking about buying that for my grandmother", Helena said. "You should", they told her. "Oh, by the way, did you write your mother and tell her about Warren? It seems strange saying his name since it turns out you knew him", Molly asked. "No, I haven't gotten up the nerve to do that, but I should soon", Helena said.

About that time, they heard Ginger, "Where are you two?" she asked. They told her they were over by the jewelry. Ginger was walking toward them. She had two bags full of stuff and a hat on her head. "Mike's going to have a fit, but I couldn't help myself. So many cute things", she said as she twirled around in a circle with her new belongings. Molly and Helena just laughed at her. "What will you tell him?". "I'll just say I got this stuff real cheap and I won't buy as much as I usually do at the commissary". The girls laughed as they headed out of the store. What a fun day. "Ginger, thanks so much for bringing us with you. It sure is a pretty island and the local people are really nice to us", Helena said. Molly spoke up and said, "Well they should be, without the military here they have nothing. The money we military spend on the island supports a lot of people". She was right.

As they were driving back to the base, Molly thanked Ginger again for taking them shopping. It was so much fun. Helena said, "I just love seeing all the interesting things on this island. Everyone says after about a year this island starts getting smaller. But everyone usually gets a chance to take a R&R trip somewhere fun like Paris". "There is a trip coming up in a few months. Why don't we get the guys to put in for the R&R?", Ginger said. "I would love that. We could do some shopping there!", Molly said. "That would be so romantic. I think Gary would like that". Helena said "A shopping and love trip. Steve and I would love seeing the sights".

A few weeks had passed, and Molly had gotten all the information for the R&R Trip to Paris. Everyone was so excited to go. The trip was planned for the middle of October which would be cold in Paris. The temperature is usually mid 80s in October on Guam.

Molly was so excited Gary could hardly keep her from talking about it all the time. Ginger was already packing; she was taking extra suitcases so she could buy some clothes. Ginger's husband Mike was so laid back. Whatever Ginger wanted, she got. Gary said he didn't think he was that laid back. He said it was just easier to let Ginger do what she wanted.

Well, the day had come. It was time. Molly couldn't help but notice that Helena seemed really nervous at the base as they waited for the plane to let them start boarding. "What's wrong Helena? Are you afraid to fly?" she asked. "Oh, no, it is not that", Helena responded. "Well, what is it?", she asked again.

Molly watched her face as it looked so sad. "That is where Andre's family is from." She finally said. "Oh, no, Helena, I never thought about that when we planned this trip.", Molly responded. "It is okay. It just brought back some memories." She said. "Did you tell Steve?", Molly asked. "No, I didn't want him to think I was thinking of the past. He is such a good husband. I know it is silly of me. I didn't know any of this family, so I am just being silly.", Helena responded. Molly began to reassure her, "No, it is okay. The past has a way no matter how hard we try. It finds a way of popping in our minds". Helena continued, "I can still close my eyes and see his beautiful face, his dark hair and those light blue eyes. I don't think I will ever forget what he looked like and the terrible way he died. I will never have closure. Everything was private. The only thing I had was his grave site."

Molly held her hand and comforted her, "'It will get better with time. You just have to move forward. Steve is there for you. Don't ever shut him out. He understands. He had a great loss too." "Yes, I know" Helena responded, "that is one of the things that brought us together. And, you of course pushing me to find love and happiness. I am so grateful for you. If it wasn't for you, Molly, I would probably still be in Massachusetts with my Grandmother and living that unproductive life." Molly smiled at her friend, "I just wanted you to be happy Helena." "Yes, Molly, I know, and I am happy thanks to you", Helena responded.

"Have you heard from your Mother?", Molly asked Helena. "Yes, I have. She mentioned she had not heard from her friend. I have been thinking about just waiting till we go back to the states to tell her about Warren. I am sure she will meet someone

34

else. She told me my dad was living with another woman and traveling with a small circus. She didn't tell me what he was doing. I am so happy to be away from that life.", Molly responded.

Everyone got in their seats and ready for their flight. Gary told Molly and Ginger they had to stop talking about what they were going to do in Paris. "Everyone can hear everything you are saying. Just sit back and relax. We have a long flight", Gary said to the girls.

Helena could feel the plane put the wheels down when the pilot came on saying they would be arriving at Orly AFB and landing shortly. The pilot buzzed on and said, "Everyone have a great week of R&R and we will see you on the return flight back to Guam next week," as they began to exit the airplane. They hoped it wouldn't take too long going through customs. "I am so excited to see our hotel room.", Moly said to Gary. "What is the name of the hotel?" Helena asked Gary too. "It is the Le Bristol Hotel.", he said. "Oh, it sounds so nice.", she answered happily. "But, let's get off this plane and get through customs and get our bags. We will catch a cab to the hotel".

A few hours had passed and finally everyone was looking for a ride to the hotel. Helena said "There is a small bus with our hotel's name on it. Let's go see if we are supposed to use it for our ride". Helena walked up to the main and said, "Bonjour". He spoke in English and said, "Hello, you people need a ride to the Le Bristol?". "Yes, we do", she said. "Get in and I will take you there". Ginger said, "look at you speaking French!". Helena laughed. "That's all I know.". They loaded on to the bus with their belongings. It was about a 20-minute drive to the hotel.

They arrived at the hotel excited and so very tired. Molly said, "As soon as we all get to our rooms lets freshen up and go get something to eat". Everyone was ready to eat; it had been a long time since lunch. Helena said, "I saw that little café next to the hotel. Let's just go there. Everyone meet in the lobby in thirty minutes". They all agreed and went their separate ways.

Molly and Gary loved their room. It had a small balcony looking out over the street. They could see the Eiffel tower. "Oh my Gary, how romantic is this? I think I am falling in love with Paris.", Molly said. "Oh Molly, you are such a hopeless romantic. That is one of the reasons I love you so much." Gary said back to her. He wrapped his arms around her and kissed her so passionately. "I love you so much.", Molly said. Gary responded, "And, I love you. Well, we better stop this right now or we will miss dinner". "Who cares about dinner!", Molly laughed. "Let's get downstairs."

After dinner everyone said goodnight. Helena and Molly had decided to go shopping tomorrow and Gary and Steve just wanted to relax, and Ginger and Mike were off to do some sightseeing. Helena told Molly, "There are all kinds of shops and stores within walking distance of the hotel. So, we can just walk. It is a lot cooler here in Paris in October, but it feels wonderful since the weather on Guam is hot and humid. Don't you just love it Molly?"

Helena said, "Look at these shops. They look like something out of a movie". Helena said, "There must be a bakery around here. I can smell bread." "Me too", Molly said. "Let's stop at the coffee café and get some coffee." They had covered several blocks window shopping. Molly had bought a few things for her sister.

As Molly and Helena sat down at the table on the street, they ordered their coffee. Helena said, "Look Molly there is the bakery. We should stop in there and take some pastries back to the hotel." Molly agreed it was a good idea. As they sat and relaxed and sipped on their coffee, Molly said, "This is so nice." As she looked over at Helena, Helena was as white as a sheet. "What is wrong Helena? Are you sick? What is it?" Molly asked her. "Molly see that man sweeping in front of the bakery?" "Yes, I see him. He is a nice-looking guy.", Molly said. "I can't believe my eyes. He looks just like Andre except a little older." Helena started to cry. "I guess my mind is playing tricks on me." "No, you are alright. It is understandable. His family was from here. Maybe it is a relative. Do you want to approach him and ask him?", Molly asked. "Oh, I couldn't do that", she said. Molly looked over at him. "Helena, he is looking at you", Molly told her. "Oh no, what should I do?", Helena asked. "We are just going to finish our coffee and then get up and walk back to the hotel".

The next day had come. It was another sunny beautiful day. No one had wanted to make plans until evening, so Helena told Steve she was just going to take a walk by herself and do a little window shopping. He was fine with that. Helena began thinking to herself "I am just going to go in the bakery. This is so silly; I have to stop this crazy thinking". When she got in front of the shop she just looked around and decided to go in. It smelled so good. Fresh baked bread and all kinds of pastries.

There was an older man behind the counter. "May I help you?", the man asked. "Yes, but I can't decide what I want.", Helena told him. He spoke broken English, but he could understand her. He pointed to some sweets and smiled. "Yes, I will take six please", she told him. He bagged them up and she paid. All the time looking around to see if she could see the guy again. As she walked out of the shop, she had a strange feeling someone was watching her. She walked a few more steps and turned around and there stood that guy from yesterday. Their eyes locked onto each other and then she heard, "Helena is that you?". Helena could not believe her eyes or ears. She could not speak. "Helena it is me Andre. What are you doing in Paris?" he asked her. She was still shocked but managed to ask him, "What are you doing? You are supposed to be dead". "What are you talking about?", he was as confused as she was now. "Your parents told me you killed yourself. I visited your grave every day for over a year", Helena explained. "My parents told me you left the states to travel with the circus and didn't ever want to see me again. I was so broken hearted", he told her. "They sent me to live here in Paris with my Uncle", he continued.

"What a horrible thing they did to you Helena. I am so sorry they were not going to let us get married. They sure went to a lot of trouble to keep us apart. I hope that made them happy. About a year after I had been here, they were killed in a car accident", he told her. "Oh, I am sorry you didn't go back home for their funeral?", she asked. "No, I really didn't have the money to travel", he responded. Andre reached for Helena's hand. "You know I have never stopped loving you. I can't believe you are here. I need to put my arms around you and hold you my sweetheart", he proclaimed. He grabbed her and held her for a minute and Helena pulled away. Helena's head was swimming around. She could not think or focus. "I am married Andre", she told him, "I have to go". "Please don't go. I want and need to talk to you. Please don't leave like this", he begged.

As Helena turned to walk away, she heard Andre say, "Please come back". Her walk turned into a run. She had to get away from him. Every feeling she ever had for Andre came rushing through her body. The tears started running down her face. "What am I going to do? Should I tell Steve?", she thought. She stopped running and then sat down on a bench outside the hotel. "I can't go in looking and feeling like this. I have got to pull myself together", her thoughts swirled in her head. Helena knew at the moment that she still had that burning love in her heart for Andre. The kind of love you only have once in your life if you are fortunate to find it. "No, I will not tell Steve. Never. He will never know that Andre is still alive", she decided to herself. Her life will go on just as planned. As she sat there composing herself, she couldn't help but think how Andre's arms felt when he wrapped them around her. Her heart was aching.

As she walked into the lobby of the hotel, everyone was there. "We have been waiting on you. We have some sight-seeing to do", they said to her. "Let's go, Paris awaits", she responded reluctantly. As they were walking out the hotel, Molly grabbed Helena's arm. "What is going on? You look like you have seen a ghost". Helena looked at her and said, "I have. I will explain later when we are by ourselves".

Chapter Five

❧

*T*HE NEXT DAY CAME. TIME WAS GOING BY FAST. ONLY A FEW DAYS left and so many more things to see. Ginger and Mike had some shopping to do. Gary and Steve were heading to the open market just to look around. So, Molly knew this would be a good time for her and Helena to talk.

Molly was heading down the hall to Helena's room when she was coming out the door. "Hey, I am coming to get you. We need to talk", Molly told her. Helena said, "Yes, we do". "What is going on with you Helena? You have not been your-self for a few days", Molly asked. "I know. I am so glad Steve has not noticed. Let's walk and talk", Helena responded.

It was a beautiful sunny day. A little cool, but it felt so nice. "Well, tell me what is going on. You looked like you had seen a ghost the other day" Molly said. "Well, Molly, in a way, I did. You will not believe this, but I saw Andre", Helena finally spilled the beans to her. "What? Andre? Do you mean you saw someone who looked like him?", Molly was confused. "No, it is really him. The guy in the bakery", Helena explained. "What? He is dead", Molly was still confused. "Well, that's what I thought. But it is him. I talked to him. I was so shocked and still am". "What did he say?", Molly asked. "His parents were so against us that they actually staged the death then sent him to Paris to live with his uncle. Then they told the story that he hung himself. I never went to the wake, so I never knew anything except for the head stone they had in the cemetery that I visited every day. They told Andre that I had left town and would never be back", Helena told her the whole story. "They sure went to a lot of trouble to keep you two apart" Molly said. "Andre said his parents were killed in a car crash last year. So, he had no reason to go back so he just stayed in Paris" Helena continued.

"Oh, Helena that is so terrible. Are you going to tell Steve?", Molly asked. "No, I will never tell him. We will leave Paris and never see him again", Helena answered. Helena started to cry. Molly put her arms around her. "It will be okay Helena", she said. "How will it ever be okay? I am married to a wonderful man. But, still in love with Andre".

A few days had passed, and it was only two days until it would be time to go back to Guam. Molly told Helena she needed to go and talk to Andre before they leave. "You need to have some closure. If not, it will haunt you the rest of your life and if you choose not to tell Steve, you have to put Andre behind you, and you will never be able to move forward", she told her.

"I know Molly. I need to see Andre before I leave. But I am afraid of what I may say", Helena said. Molly responded, "Don't be afraid Helena. Tell him how you feel". Helena was thankful to have some guidance from her friend. She told her, "You always give me your advice Molly. I will walk down in the morning when the guys are having coffee and planning out the day".

The next morning Helena woke early. She had not slept well. All she could think about was Andre. She felt so bad. She did not want to hurt Steve. He was a wonderful guy and he had helped her to put her life back together. He understood her, knowing the loss she felt from losing Andre and feels as though she can never tell him that Andre is alive because he knew the love she had for him. Our marriage would never be the same. But she would be leaving Paris soon and this would all be left in Paris. She and Steve would continue their life and she would grow to love him. He so deserved that.

As she left the hotel and was walking down to the bakery, she just prayed. "Dear Lord, let me say the right words to Andre so we both can go on with our lives". Her heart was pounding in her chest. She had a strange feeling in her body. She knew deep down inside she still loved Andre. She wanted to be in his arms and tell him she loved him. She could remember the last time they kissed. "How am I going to keep myself from letting him know how I feel?", she thought to herself. As she got to the front of the bakery, she panicked. I can't do this. It hurts too bad. She started to turn and run, but Andre stepped out of the shop. "Helena, I am so glad you came back", he said to her. Tears were in his eyes. "We need to go somewhere and talk please. I have to talk to you. Come into the shop. My cousin can take care of things. Follow me, there is an office back here", he continued.

Helena followed Andre. He closed the door behind them. "Here, sit down before you fall down. I am so sorry Helena that you found out about me like this. But I am so glad to know the truth. If you had not come to Paris, we would have never known the awful things my parents did", he told her.

"I have never stopped loving you Helena. You were the only woman for me. I felt like we were soul mates. I could not understand why you would leave me. But now I know the story. My parents tried to set me up with a French girl, but I told her I was still in love with you. My parents would get so upset with me. They would say that gypsy girl was no good for you. But I knew that you loved me Helena. Our love was so unforgettable and true", Andre continued as Helena sat in silence.

Helena stood up. Finally, she started to respond, "I must go Andre. But I wanted you to know that our love was special, and I will always love you. But I am married to a wonderful guy and he knows about us. I will not tell him about our meeting. I will go back to Guam and then in a few years, back home to Massachusetts and live a happy life. I hope you will find happiness too". As Helena was talking, Andre started walking toward her. He reached out and pulled her into him. She could not resist him. He pressed his lips against hers. It seemed like the earth stopped spinning for a moment. The love she felt for him in that moment was indescribable. She pulled away from him and insisted that he listen to her, "Andre, Stop! Listen to me. I will never ever stop loving you. Please remember that. But I have a wonderful life and you need to move on. There will be an ocean between us. I am so glad to know you are alive and what we had will always be in our hearts. But it is the past and we have to go forward living in the future. I will never forget you Andre". As Helena turned to walk away, Andre grabbed her hand putting something in it and told her, "I was planning on giving you this when we were to see each other, but my parents didn't let that happen. Please never forget me".

Helena clinched her fist as she turned and hurried out of the bakery. Tears were running down her face. Her heart aching, she wanted to run back into his arms, but knowing that was impossible. As she got closer to the hotel, she knew she had to pull herself together knowing Steve would be there waiting on her. She felt a little sick at her stomach with so many feelings running through her head. She loved Steve. He is such a wonderful guy and they have planned a great life together and that's what she wanted to have. He will never know about this encounter with Andre. It will stay here in Paris, she convinced herself.

The next day passed quickly as they had to get ready to get their flight back to Guam. Helena stayed very busy so she would not think of Andre.

There was a knock on the door. Steve yelled out, "I will get it. Hurry up Helena I know everyone is waiting on us". He answered the door and announced, "It is Molly, Helena. Everyone is downstairs". "Go ahead Steve", Molly said, "We will be right down". Steve headed out the door. Molly took Helena by the hand and looked at her in the eyes. "It will be fine Helena. We will get back to Guam and your life will go on as usual", she reassured her.

A couple months had passed, and it was getting close to Christmas. Helena couldn't imagine Christmas on Guam. Molly and Helena had been doing some shopping. Molly asked Helena, "Don't you just love this weather? It is sunny and beautiful". Helena responded, "Yes, Molly, it is warm, but I like it". "Have you sent your Christmas gifts back to the states?", Molly asked full of excitement for the Christmas season. "No, I am not sending anything just some cards. I only hear from my Grandmother. I don't know what is going on with my mother", Helena told her. "Oh, that is too bad. I sent a big box of stuff to my family about a month ago. My sisters will love all the crazy island things. I should be getting a box from my family pretty soon", Molly told Helena. "You are so lucky to have a family Molly. People who love and care about you", Helena responded.

A few weeks had passed. Helena had gotten a letter from her grandmother.

> *Helena,*
> *Winter is cold and snowy in Massachusetts and I am doing fine. I am staying very busy with my palm reading. The base is full of airmen with the war going on in Vietnam. Hoping you are happy Helena in your new life.*
>
> *Love,*
> *Grandmother*

Helena missed her grandmother. She was really the only family she had. Her mother and father always lived their own life and that never included Helena.

Christmas was only a week away. It was so strange to see Christmas decorations up with it so hot. Even palm trees were decorated. Molly has received a package from her family and a note from her Daddy ...

> *Merry Christmas Molly,*
> *Hope you and Gary are fine. It is cold here, but no*
> *snow. Everyone said to say Hi. Thinking of you my*
> *daughter. Write when you can.*
>
> *Love always,*
> *Your Dad*

Molly loved hearing from her Daddy. He never said a lot, but she knew how much he loved her. He took great care of her mother and sisters and bother. His family came first.

Christmas day had arrived. Everyone was coming over to Molly and Gary's place. The little tree was up and the gifts under the tree. Helena and Steve had arrived first. Ginger and Mike were running a little later. Gary had baked a small turkey with all the trimmings. Helena admired, "It smells so good in here. I am not used to this. We never celebrated Christmas at my house". About that time, Ginger came in the house and exclaimed, "Merry Christmas everyone!". She had baked a cake in the shape of a Christmas tree. Helena teased, "I hope that tastes as good as it looks".

The day had come to an end. Everyone was heading home. Ginger thanked Molly for a great dinner and day. "When you can't be with family, your friends become your family and to be halfway around the world, this was just great", Ginger said thankfully. Everyone said goodnight. Gary looked at Molly and said, "That was a good time, but my best present of all is you. I love you Molly". She responded back, "And I love you Gary". "Let's call it a night. I have to be at the base early in the morning. They are bringing in more B-B2 planes. There is so much action going on in Vietnam. I am so grateful I am here on this rock they call Guam. Steve said, he might have to do a short trip to Vietnam. He hasn't told Helena yet. Don't say anything to her. Steve will tell her. I think it is only a few days. Everything is top secret in the military", Gary told Molly.

Gary asked Molly, "Do you think Helena already knows? She seemed quiet today". "I don't think so. Maybe just missing her grandmother it being her first time away from home. Even though she lived a very strange life, she does love her grandmother", Molly explained to Gary. "Well, let's get some sleep. Thanks for a wonderful Christmas Molly. I love you and sweet dreams", he responded. Gary Pulled her into his arms holding her close as they fell asleep.

Chapter Six

&

A MONTH HAS PASSED, AND ANOTHER YEAR HAD ROLLED AROUND. Everything was going pretty normal. The guys were busy at the base. They didn't talk much about the fighting in Vietnam. Molly and Helena spent a lot of time together. They had a great social life with the other wives on the base.

Helena was having a glass of iced tea and writing a letter to her grandmother when she looked up and there stood Molly. "Hi Helena. What are you doing?", Molly asked. "Not much. Come on in" Helena responded happy to see her friend. "I decided I wanted to walk over and see what you were doing today", Molly told her. "Just writing this letter to my grand-mother", Helena told her. Molly asked if she was going to tell her about seeing Andre. "Oh, no, I told you I would never tell anyone. You are the only one who knows. I am trying to forget I ever saw him, but it is so hard. Can I show you something Molly?", she responded. Molly agreed to look. "I was storing some things in the suitcase the other day and I found something. Wait a minute. I will show you". She left the room for a minute then returned. "When I was saying goodbye to Andre, he grabbed my hand and put something in it. I guess I was so upset I threw it in the suitcase and forgot about it". "What is it Helena, show me?", Molly was curious. Helena opened up her hand. "It is a necklace", Helena told her. "Yes, it is, and it says Forever on it", Molly noticed. "Andre told me he was planning on giving it to me, but that never happened. What am I to do with it? Every time I hold it in my hand, I know I will never stop loving him", Helena announced.

Molly put her hand on Helena's shoulder. "Look at me. It is Okay. Yes, your love will be unforgettable, but you can move forward. God has allowed you to see Andre and so you can put this behind you. Take the necklace and put it away. It is a piece of your past. Maybe someday you will be able to tell Steve about this, but until that day, move forward letting the love you have for Steve grow stronger. You have an ocean between you and Andre". Helena was sad but knew she was right; she must move forward.

A few months had passed, and things were going well. Helena had put the Paris trip behind her. She and Steve were enjoying their life together. Steve was such a good husband to Helena. They even talked about starting a family one day. Helena and Molly had become as close as sisters. They even talked about living close to each other when the guys got out of the air force. But Helena knew Steve wanted to enlist again after his four years were up. Helena knew she and Molly would remain friends forever no matter where they lived.

A few weeks had passed, and the rainy season had come. It was still hot and humid, but it would rain a little every day. Molly and Helena had planned a day at the beach. Ginger had made plans with another friend so she couldn't go. Steve told Helena they would probably get rained on, but she didn't care. The beach was so pretty. She loved to watch the waves roll in. It was a beautiful day at the beach. Not too crowded. The coconut palms lined the beach. Helena had never seen anything like this. She loved the ocean breeze and the smell of the air. It just made her feel so alive. Molly said, "Let's put the blanket down here under this palm tree". Helena agreed, "I hope a coconut doesn't fall on us. That would be terrible". They both laughed. "Let's get in the water Helena". "Okay, but only to my knees", Helena agreed. The water was warm and was so pretty and blue. What a great way to spend a day.

Molly and Helena were alike in so many ways. A lot of people thought they were sisters. They even looked alike. As they were sitting on the beach enjoying the sun, Molly asked Helena, "Don't you find it strange that we became friends?". "Yes, I tried everything to not talk to you, but you would not leave me alone". "Then, your grandmother telling me about my father and then finding out that he was your mother's friend. And, that you knew him". "I still have a hard time understanding that. Not knowing the whole story". "Yes, but you did get to see him. You didn't know it was him at the time". "Yes, this is true, but you know Helena, I felt something when I looked at him. It was a very strange feeling and I think by the way he looked at me, he did too", Molly said. ""But, Molly, you are so lucky to have a wonderful dad like you have", Helena remarked. "Yes Helena, He is wonderful. I don't think I could have loved Warren more than my dad and I know he loved me. But you know there is a feeling you have when you know someone doesn't want you. It's hard to explain", Molly continued. "I understand Molly. My father was around sometimes, but he loved the traveling circus life more than my mother than me. I guess that is why my mother enjoyed the guys from the base, but I think Warren was her favorite. He was nice but seemed so very sad. Maybe he told her about you. When I get back to the states, I will ask her. She might know his side of the story Molly", Helena said. Molly responded, "I am glad our paths crossed. We have so much in common, but, yet different too".

Time was passing quickly on Guam. Their time was almost half over. The guys had gotten really busy on the base with the war going on in Vietnam. They were on alert at all times. The B52 bomber flew out of Anderson AFB over to Vietnam. There were rumors that some were going to be sent on a temporary duty assignment to Vietnam. No one was looking forward to that.

Another beautiful day had rolled around. Helena had just come in from getting the mail. There was a letter from her grandmother. She was so happy to see it. She opened it quickly.

Dear Helena,
Hope this finds you well and happy. I am doing okay.
Slowing down a bit, but that is fine. The years do that
to you. Summer has come again in New England,
but I guess you have summer all year in Guam.

I heard from your Mother last week. She said she is
traveling with a small carnival. She said she's fine

*and asked me if she had gotten any mail. I think she
is looking for a letter from that airman that she likes
so much.*

Take care of yourself. Write when you can.

As always,
Grandmother

Helena was so happy to hear from her Grandmother. She wished she could tell her grandmother about Andre, but she knew she couldn't. Molly is the only person that will ever know. Her mind drifted back to Paris. She could still feel Andre's arms around her. She was so grateful to know he was alive, but so sad to know she will live the rest of her life loving him in her heart. She felt the tears coming when she heard the door open. "Hi Honey, you home?". She wiped the tears away and ran to Steve. "So glad to see you. I missed you today Helena", Steve told her. "I missed you", she responded. Steve noticed her eyes were a little puffy and red and asked, "Have you been crying?". She explained, "Oh, I got a letter from my grandmother today. Just a little sad, that's all". Steve told her to come sit down and said, "I want to tell you what is going on at the base".

"Well, Helena, it looks like in a couple months they will be sending half of the squadron to a base in Vietnam. They need some jet mechanics on the base over there", he told her reluctantly. "Oh no Steve! Will you have to go?", Helena questioned. "I don't know yet. They will be posting a list in about a week or so", he told her. "How long will they have to be there?" Helena had so many questions. "I don't know yet", he responded.

Helena started to cry. Her day kept getting worse. Steve told her it was alright and assured her that he didn't know if he would even have to go or not. "What about Gary? Does Molly know about this?", Helena asked. "I think Gary was going to tell her today. Please don't worry about it Helena. It will be alright", he told her. Steve held her in his arms. "This is part of being in the military". Helena looked up at Steve. "I love you Steve and I am so happy that you came into my life". He told her that he loved her to and reminded her not to get too sad, since they didn't know what was going to happen.

A few weeks had gone by and everything was going great. The girls had joined a card club and were having lots of fun and meeting lots of nice women. Helena loved the fact that these women were from everywhere and different in their own way. No one cared that she was from a gypsy family.

Helena had asked Molly if she wanted to go do a little shopping at the Bx. She had a little extra money and Molly agreed and told her she would pick her up. Gary was riding into work with one of the guys so she would have the car. "We can treat ourselves to a hamburger at the hamburger shack", the two agreed.

Helena and Molly were shopping at the Bx finding some really good sales. The base seemed to be really busy and lots more people than normal. Molly asked Helena, "Where did all of the people come from?". "I don't know, but I bet it has something to do with some of them being transferred to Vietnam. I sure hope our guys don't have to go. What will we do?". Helena told Molly, "We will just have to wait and pray. Since it will be a temporary duty, we will stay here on Guam till they come back". The two continued their shopping, got a treat at the hamburger shack, and headed home.

Well, the day had come, and the list was posted. The guys all took turns looking to see who was going to Vietnam for a three-week TDY. "It looks like they have taken half of the squadron", Gary told Steve as he stepped back to let Steve look.

Steve got a knot in his stomach when he looked at the list. "It looks like I will be going", Steve told Gary. The two looked at each other and knew how hard it would be on Helena. "When are you going to tell Helena?", Gary asked. "Just as soon as I get home. She will not be happy, but she knows this is how the Air Force works. Three weeks is not that long, and I know Molly will keep her busy while I am gone. At least we both didn't get orders to go", Steve responded. "Yes, that is true. That would have been hard on the girls", Gary said.

Steve sat Helena down and told her as soon as he got home. Helena was trying to be strong for Steve. She knew this was his job. They only had a week and he would be shipping out. Steve told Helena, "It will be just a few weeks and I will be back on this rock. The time will go fast I promise you".

"Molly will keep you busy", he continued. "I know she will, but I am so afraid for you Steve. That war is so bad", she worried. "Yes, it is Helena, but the Air Force doesn't fight like the Army and Marines. I should be pretty safe. Just doing some repairs on the planes. Everything will be alright. I love you Helena", he reassured her. "And I love you Steve", she responded.

A few days had passed. Everything was going on as normal as it could. Molly and Gary were spending the last few days with Steve and Helena. They knew Helena was having a hard time. The day had come way too quickly for Helena. But it was early Monday morning. Steve stood at the front door with Helena. Steve held her in his arms. "It will be okay. I will be back before you know it", he told her. Helena started to cry. "Please don't cry. This is my job. You know how much I love you and I am so grateful you came into my life. Always remember that", Steve told his wife. "I will Steve. I love you", Helena responded. He turned and went out the door. Helena had such a sick feeling in her heart. She had felt that feeling before.

A couple weeks had passed. Helena had kept herself busy. Molly was on her way over. They were going to go do a little shopping. It was a beautiful day on Guam. Helena checked her mailbox while she was outside waiting on Molly. There was a letter from her grandmother. She opened it quickly. She loved hearing from her. They were always short letters, but so sweet.

> *Dear Helena,*
> *I hope you are doing well. I have had several dreams about you lately. I know you don't believe in my dreams, but I feel like Steve is in danger …*

Helena dropped the letter. Oh my! Her heart started to pound. She just stood there looking at the letter on the ground.

Molly pulled up and said, "Helena what is going on? Your letter is on the ground". Molly bent down and picked it up. "Here, Helena". "No, I can't read it. You read it to me Molly", she told her. Molly agreed. "Just start where it says Steve is in danger, please".

Helena, prepare yourself. Something is going to happen, but you will be alright.

"Stop reading Molly! I don't want to hear any more", she blurted out. "Why would she say such a thing?", Helena questioned. "I guess she thinks you need to know", Molly responded unsure of what else to say. Helena started to cry. "Don't cry, it is okay. Steve will be back in about a week. Let's go shopping and take your mind off of everything", Molly assured her. Molly felt a little upset about the remarks Helena's grandmother made. She couldn't stop thinking about what she told her about Warren. Molly just prayed, "Please God, let Steve be okay".

They finished shopping and Molly dropped Helena back at her house. Molly hugged Helena and comforted her, "It will be okay Helena. Please don't worry. I will talk to you tomorrow". Helena said, "Thanks Molly. You are always looking out for me". As Molly drove away, she couldn't help but think, what if something happens to Steve?

When Molly got home, Gary was already home. She walked in the door and Gary's eyes met hers. She knew something was wrong. "What is it Gary? It is Steve", she fretted. "Oh no!", she exclaimed. She could read him so well he didn't even have to respond. "His helicopter went down as they were coming back to Guam", he told her. "What happened?", she was in shock. "They think engine failure. No one survived the crash" he reluctantly told her. "Oh, dear God! When will they tell Helena?", Molly was worried about her best friend. "Probably tomorrow morning. They will be bringing back the bodies to Guam", he explained. "Poor Helena! We need to be there when they tell her", Molly declared. "The Air Force is trying to keep it quiet until all the families have been notified. There are eight families", he continued. "This is so sad Gary". Molly started to cry. "I am so grateful you did not have to go. War is terrible". "Yes, it is" he agreed. Gary held Molly close.

The next day came and Gary told Molly, he was going to come pick her up and they would go to Helena's together. They will be at her house today to inform her and they wanted to be there with her. "I am going to tell her myself about Steve. She is too good of a friend", Molly had decided. "I have to let her know".

Helena heard the knock on the door. She looked up from the kitchen where she was having her breakfast. She saw Gary and Molly. Her heart skipped a beat. She knew something was not right. As she answered the door, she said, "What is it?" she asked. Gary reached for her. Helena knew. "No, no, this can't be happening! Not Steve!", she broke down. "I am so sorry Helena. Steve's helicopter went down a few miles off Guam on their way back. There were no survivors, but they did recover all the bodies", Molly told her friend choking back tears. Helena started to cry, "I can't believe Steve is gone". Molly held Helena. "I am so sorry Helena. It just isn't fair. Steve was such a good guy". "What do I do now Gary?", Helena asked. "Well, the air force will send a representative and a chaplain this afternoon to make arrangements", he told her. "Do I get to see him?" Helena was crying so hard; she could hardly speak. "I don't know how that works, but I do know they will be sending his body back to Westover AFB and you will have to go too", he explained. "Oh, what am I going to do without you two?", she asked. "Maybe I can go with her Gary", Molly said. "I don't know Molly that is a lot of money. We will have to talk about it", he responded.

Helena asked Molly, "Will you stay here with me until the Air Force comes and tells me what is going on?". "Of course, I will", Molly told her. Gary said his goodbyes and told Molly he would come back and ger her when he gets off work. "Maybe we will know a little more by then", he hoped.

The doorbell rang. Helena walked to the door. She could see two air force men standing there. As she opened the door for them to come in, her life flashed in front of her and all the heartache in it. "Mrs. Cliff, we are here to inform you that Steve Cliff has been killed in active duty. His helicopter went down on a small island as they were approaching Guam. His body has been recovered. We are so sorry for your loss. Sergeant Cliff served his country to the fullest and we thank you for his service", they handed her a letter. "You will need to come in and identify the body". Helena just stood there lost in the moment. She watched as the two men walked away.

Molly went to Helena and hugged her. "It will be okay. Read the letter Helena". She opened it up. As she read it, Molly could see the tears in her eyes. She closed it very slowly and looked at Molly. "I have to leave the base next Friday and go with Steve's body back to Westover AFB. I am going to bury him at home. I have so much to do" she sighed. "The Air Force will help you. All you need to do is tell them what you want", Molly did her best to comfort her.

Friday had rolled around; the week went by so fast. Helena was so sad to leave Molly. What would happen now? Steve is gone. Helena held on to Molly. "You have always been there for me", Helena said. "I know Helena. My heart is breaking too. I promise when we leave Guam, we will come see you", Molly promised. "At least I have my grandmother. I am going to bury Steve in the cemetery that I spent so much time in thinking Andre was buried there. Isn't it strange how things happen? I just can't seem to wrap my head around it".

Molly and Gary drove Helena to the airplane that was taking Steve's body back. The flag draped casket was more than they could bare. They cried as they said their goodbyes. Molly grabbed Helena's hand. "Please write soon". Helena headed up the stairs of the plane. She was accompanied by an air man to help her. It was a little comfort, but not much. The flight would be long. Helena thought to herself, "Please God, just let me get his body home and buried".

Helena didn't think the plane would ever land. She had so much to think about. Steve didn't have any family so she thought she would have a private gravesite burial at the cemetery that she spent so much time at. The Air Force had a touching ceremony for all the guys that lost their lives in the helicopter crash. So, it was time to bury his body and let him rest in peace.

A few weeks passed and things were calming down. Helena was happy to see her grandmother. Helena was missing Molly so bad. She hoped she would get to see her again someday. Helena and her grandmother would have long talks about all that had happened. She wanted to tell her that Andre was alive and living in Paris, but she would never forget the love she had for him. She was so sad. She loved Steve in a different way. He was a great husband, but her heart would always belong to Andre.

Helena knew she could stay with her grandmother for a while, but she wanted to find an apartment and get on with her life. She needed a job. It was hard watching all the air force guys coming to get their fortunes told.

The weeks went by fast. Helena found a job at a small deli about a mile from her grandmother. She could walk the distance even if it was snowing and winter was already there. No snow yet, but it was coming. New England always had a long winter.

The deli was family owned by a sweet polish couple named Stella and Nick. Helena knew they would get along just fine. The deli is close to a college, so they are really busy which is what Helena wanted to keep her mind off of everything that had happened. Stella had given her a couple uniforms, so she was ready to start to work on Monday.

Monday came with a light snow and cold, but Helena made it to work at the deli without any trouble. There was something so peaceful about her walk to work. The snow falling was beautiful and she felt it against her face like God was refreshing her and letting her know it was going to be alright. She would grieve the loss of Steve, but she was so grateful he had come into her life. She would always love him for that. She had grown so much in life since the days of going to the cemetery to visit Andre's grave. It was time to start a new chapter in her life and this job would get her started in the right direction.

Chapter Seven

A FEW WEEKS HAD PASSED, AND THINGS COULD NOT BE ANY BETTER. The job was working out great. The deli was very busy, and time went by fast. Stella was very nice to Helena. They got along very well. Stella knew Helena's husband had been killed overseas. Helena had told her some of her life, but not all of it. Stella did know that her grandmother was the fortune teller that lived in town. Everyone knew about the gypsy's fortune teller. Helena loved her grandmother. She was really the only one that raised her. She didn't really believe that she could see the future, but she had said a lot of things that had happened. Her grandmother called it a gift that she could see things. Helena thought it was a way to make money off of the guys and people at the AFB.

Helena had gotten a letter from Molly. She was so glad to hear from her. She missed her so much. Molly said things were going fine and Gary was busy at the base working a lot of hours keeping those planes in the air. It was so hot, and she did miss some of the snow and cold, but not much. Molly said she hoped and prayed that Gary would be sent back to Westover AFB before he got out of the air force so she and Helena could see one another again. Hopefully the next eighteen months would go by fast.

A few weeks had passed, and the weather had set in with lots of snow. One of the ladies from the deli was picking Helena up in the morning so she didn't have to walk in the snow. Her name was Colleen.

Colleen was an older woman who was Irish and had liked Helena right away. She was wise enough to know that Helena had a story. Colleen had worked at the deli for fifteen years. She and her husband have always lived in Wilbraham, Massachusetts. She had wondered if Helena was the gypsy girl that was in love with the French boy. That was such a sad story. Colleen really liked Helena. She would never ask about it. Colleen knew Helena's husband had been killed in a helicopter crash overseas and Helena was trying to make a life for herself.

Several months had passed and Helena liked working in the deli. She had saved quite a bit of money since she was living with her grandmother and the air force had sent her a check for Steve being killed. So, she knew it was time to find a place of her own. She had never lived by herself but was ready. There were lots of apartments because of the AFB so she knew it would be easy to find one. She needed to get a few pieces of furniture. Colleen told her she would be happy to go with her apartment and furniture shopping.

Helena knew her grandmother would be upset but it was time to leave her house and try and start a life on her own. Helena and Colleen planned to go apartment hunting on Saturday. They didn't work on Saturday. Helena was excited to go look and see what she could find. They looked all day, but nothing seemed to work. As they were driving back, they passed a bakery. Colleen said, "I love this bakery. Do you care if we stop and pick up some fresh bread?". Helena responded, "No, that is fine. I might get something for myself".

As she walked in the bakery, she could smell the wonderful aroma of the baked goods and for a minute she was back in Paris where she saw Andre. Her heart hurt for a minute. The unforgettable love she has for him; it made her so sad. Colleen could see Helena's body language shift, "What is the matter Helena?". Helena snapped out of it, "Oh, nothing. I was just thinking what I wanted". "Well, you looked like you were a thousand miles away" Colleen remarked.

The man behind the counter filled their bags. "This is really a nice shop", Helena said. "Yes, it is. I stop here when I am over this way. They have a really good business", Colleen explained. As they were walking out the door, Helena saw a sign that said apartment for rent. She looked at Colleen and said, "Should I ask about it?". "Well, the location would be good", Colleen agreed. Helena walked back to the counter and said, "Excuse me, could I ask about the apartment that you have for rent?". The man said, "Of course. It is four rooms. Would you like to see it?". Helena was pleasantly surprised it had that much space, "Oh, yes, that would be great".

"The apartment is upstairs in the back of the store". The man yelled at the girl in the back and told her to watch the counter. "I'm going to show the apartment", he told the girl. He said, "Follow me", in broken English. He sounded like he was French. Helena put out her hand, "I am Helena Cliff. Nice to meet you". "I am Mack", he responded, "Are you air force young lady?". Helena answered, "No sir, I am not, it is just me".

As they were climbing the steps, Colleen said laughing, "You would never go hungry living over a bakery". Helena just smiled. "You are right!". Helena liked the apartment. It has some furniture in it which would work out great. It was small, but really perfect for her. "I think I would like to rent it, Mr. Mack, if I could" she told the man. "Do you have any references?", he asked. "Oh, yes. I work for Stella and Nick Luck over at the Sunshine Deli", she told him. "I know who they are. If you work for them that is good enough for me. Wouldn't you like to know the price of the rent?" he chuckled and asked. "Oh, yes, I do", she said. He told her it was $75 a month and they agreed on it. "When can I move in?", Helena asked. "Well, if you want to pay your rent today, then I will give you a key and it is all yours", Mr. Mack told her. "That's what I want to do", Helena was excited. "Okay let's go downstairs and we will take care of the paperwork".

Helena was so excited. "I will help you move", Colleen said, "My car is big enough to get a lot in it". Colleen told Helena, "That would be great. I don't have a lot of things, but enough to get started". Helena finished the paperwork and Colleen dropped her off at her grandmothers. She knew her grandmother would be sad, but she knew it was time to get on with her life.

A few hours had passed, and Helena had all her belongings on the porch waiting for Colleen to pick her up. Colleen pulled up and Helena started carrying her things to the car. "Thank you so much for doing this for me", Helena told her. "I am happy to help. Was it hard leaving your grandmother?", she asked. "No, it was okay. I was gone for a few years, so it was easier this time", she explained. They got everything carried up the stairs. Helena was so happy to be there. "Let's get your sheets on the bed", Colleen said. "That sounds good. I am going to sleep here now and for a long time", Helena announced.

Colleen had carried in a basket and put it on the table for Helena. "What is in the basket?", Helena asked realizing it was not hers. "That is your dinner and some food for breakfast", Colleen told her. "Oh, Colleen you are so thoughtful. I had not even thought of eating, but I will when I finish unpacking, I will be hungry!", Helena was thankful. Colleen told Helena goodbye and told her that she would pick her up for work on Monday.

Helena got busy putting things away. It was a small apartment but is all she needed. She wished Molly was there, but she knew she could do this. Another chapter in her life, but she just had to keep moving forward.

A few weeks had passed, and it was still cold and snowing but Spring would come. Helena told Colleen that she was happy in the apartment. She felt blessed to have a place to live and a job. Helena kept Steve's picture on the table beside her bed. She missed him so much. She could hear him say, "It will be okay my gypsy girl". If only she could believe that. Steve always made her feel better. He knew that Helena loved before him and he understood that some loves are unforgettable.

Winter was slowly leaving. Helena could hardly wait until Spring. She was hoping to get a letter from Molly saying they would be coming back to Westover after leaving Guam. Helena looked forward to getting off work today and go home and check her mail. She left a little early and she told Colleen she needed to walk today. Colleen said, "It has warmed up a little. Be careful. See you tomorrow".

Helena walked and thought about her life. She couldn't keep from thinking about Andre. It seems like a dream that she ran into him in Paris. She had tried so hard to forget him, but their love was so strong.

As she reached the apartment, she could tell she had mail. It was a letter from Molly. As Helena read the letter, she began to cry. She misses Molly so much. She had become like a sister to her. As she read the letter, she got so excited. Molly said they would be coming back to Westover in May and Gary's squadron would rotate out. Helena grabbed a piece of paper to answer Molly's letter. She was so happy to hear the news.

> *Dear Molly,*
> *So happy to hear from you. Can't wait until you get here. I have rented a nice little apartment and my job at the deli is going well. The couple I work for are so nice to me.*
>
> *Please stay with me at my apartment if Gary doesn't have housing for you guys yet. Write soon*

*and let me know when you will get here. At least
it will be Springtime.*

Your friend Always,
Helena

A month had passed and not as much snow was on the ground anymore. Things were good at the deli. Helena loved her job. There were so many nice people that came in the store. Stella and Nick always had a little gift basket for her at the end of the week when she got her check. Stella wanted to make sure Helena had something to eat.

One day while Helena was working behind the counter slicing up some meat and cheese, a man came in and was looking around. "Can I help you sir?", she asked. "Why, yes, is Stella or Nick around?", he asked. "No, I am sorry they took the afternoon off. Could I help you?", she told him. "No, I am a friend of theirs and just wanted to say Hi and see how they are", he explained. "They are doing well. Who should I tell them was here?", she asked. "Oh, I am Bill Costello. Tell them I will try and see them again soon when I am on this side of town" he said.

"I will tell them", Helena said. "I guess while I am here, I should get some of Stella's homemade sausage and cabbage" the man told her. "Sure, I will wrap it up for you". "How long have you worked here young lady?", he asked her. She told him she had worked there for a few months. "I guess your husband is in the air force?", he asked. Helena's heart skipped a beat. "No, he is not, he was killed in a helicopter crash while we were overseas", she reluctantly responded. "Oh, I am so very sorry" he responded. "Thank you, but I am okay. I came back home to try and put my life back together", she told him. "So, you do have family here?", he continued with the questions. "Only a grandmother, but I am getting along fine. Stella and Nick have been great to me", she told him. "If I can ever help you" he started. "Oh, I don't even know your name". "It's Helena. Nice to meet you", she said. "I am Father Bill Costello.", he told her. "You're a priest?", she questioned. "Yes, I am. I have a small church a few blocks away from here", he explained. "I walk past it when I came to work", Helena knew exactly where he was talking about. "You walk to work?", he asked. "Yes, I do except when it is really cold. Then, my friend Colleen picks me up", she responded. "That's good. I know Colleen. She has worked here a long time. If you ever need anything Helena, stop by the church. I am always around somewhere". He patted her on the hand as he walked away. What a nice guy, Helena thought. I would have never guessed him to be a priest.

Time was going by fast. Spring was coming. Still snow on the ground, but the temperature was getting warmer every day. Easter would soon be here. Then, the next month Molly and Gary would be there.

As Helena was walking home one evening from work, she decided to stop at St. Michael Church where Father Bill was. It was very quiet. Only a couple people were there praying. It was a beautiful old Catholic church. Helena crossed herself as she kneeled down. She had such a peaceful feeling. She had not been to church for a long time.

She felt someone touch her on the shoulder. As she looked around, she saw Father Bill. He smiled and said, "So nice to see you Helena". "Could I stop by some time Father Bill? I have a few questions I would like to ask you", she told him. "Yes, any time Helena", he responded.

Chapter Eight

A month had passed, and Helena was looking forward to Molly and Gary coming. They would arrive in a couple weeks. Helena had been thinking about Andre so much. She wished she could stop. She knew she would never see him again. She knew she needed to talk to someone. Father Bill kept coming into her mind. I will stop by and see if he has time to talk, she thought to herself.

Sunday had rolled around. It was a beautiful Spring day. The air was cool, but the sun was so bright. The flowers were beginning to peak through the ground. As she walked to church, she knew she had to talk to Father Bill after mass.

When mass was over, she just stayed in her pew trying to figure out what to say. Father Bill walked back to her and smiled. "Hi Helena. You look like you have something on your mind". "I do Father Bill. I need to talk about something that happened in my life a few years ago. I fell in love with a guy. He was my soulmate. We had planned to marry and make a wonderful life together", she started to explain. "So, what happened Helena?", he asked. "He was French, and my family are gypsies. His family would not accept me. We tried everything we could to convince them that we were right for one another.

We loved each other so much", she continued. Helena started to cry. Father Bill tried to comfort her, "Don't cry Helena. I remember hearing about this story. It was so tragic. He took his own life, didn't he?". "Well, that was the story they told. They didn't have a funeral. They only told me he hung himself. I was heartbroken and devastated. I felt like my life was over. I went to the cemetery every day trying to find an answer for why this happened", she explained.

"I had a friend help me get my life back together. I am so grateful to her. I did marry to a great guy. But he was killed in a helicopter crash and that brought me back home to Massachusetts. But, Father Bill, here's the problem. While I was over in Paris with my late husband, I saw Andre. He was working in his uncle's bakery. I could not believe my eyes. We talked only for a moment. He said his parents had faked his death and they told him I had moved out of state. So, they hated me being a gypsy so much they would send their only son away to another country to keep us from getting married", she told him everything. "That is such a sad story. I remember hearing a little about that. What a shock it must have been to run into

Andre", he said. "Yes, for the both of us. It made my heart hurt. Some loves are unforgettable. I never told Steve, my late husband. He knew all about that part of my life. He was a wonderful guy. He helped me put my life back together", she told Father Bill.

Helena looked at her watch. "Oh my, Father, I have been talking way too long. I am so sorry". "That's okay Helena. What I do best is listen to people. Please feel free to stop by any time. I have enjoyed our talk. Be careful walking home".

A few weeks passed. Helena was getting so excited. Molly and Gary would be at Westover in about a week. Things were going well at the deli. She loved her apartment. Helena was making a new life for herself and it was good. Father Bill had helped her so much to accept the things that had happened in her life.

Helena would visit her grandmother about once a month, but she never enjoyed it. She was always busy with her fortune telling. So many air force guys coming and going. It would bring back a lot of memories. The last time Helena visited her grandmother she told her there is love coming back in your life. She told her grandmother not to say that, she couldn't handle it.

The time had come. Helena was excited. Molly and Gary were coming in tonight. She had asked Father Bill if he could drive her to the base to pick them up. Father Bill couldn't keep from laughing at Helena. "You are like a child at Christmas", he said. He knew how much Molly and Gary meant to her.

They got to the base just in time. The plane had landed. "Follow me Father Bill" she told him. Helena was almost in a run. "Slow down Helena" he said to her while laughing. Father Bill could see the passengers getting off the plane. Then, he heard Helena yell, "Molly!", in a half-cracked voice. She ran to meet her. They hugged and hugged. Gary was laughing as Father Bill came up to them. "You must be Father Bill, I am Gary. Helena has told us all about you", Gary said. "Nice to meet you", Father Bill responded. Gary told Father Bill, "They will come up for air in a minute. Lots of tears of joy right there.

It sure feels good to be back at Westover. That rock was getting pretty small". Helena turned around to give Gary a hug. "Molly, this is Father Bill". "So nice to meet you", Molly said to him. "Let's get going to my apartment", Helena said. Gary spoke up and said, "Helena, I have to check in at the base so they will know I have arrived". Helena knew the drill and responded, "We will go get a cup of coffee at the café while you do that. That will give us a little time to get acquainted".

Helena and Molly were so excited to see one another. Father Bill told Molly, "I am so happy that you are here. Helena was very home sick for you. She shared a lot with me about how the two of you met". "Yes, Father Bill, we have had a very interesting journey. I feel like God put her in my life to lead me to a lot of unanswered questions in my own life and in return we have helped each other and become lifelong friends. I am happy that she has met you and is moving forward in her life. Now, speaking about you, I'm not one to beat around the bush. How come such a young nice-looking man", Father Bill started to laugh, he knew what she was about to ask. "Helena told me you would want to know my life story", he responded. "Well, then, what is your story? Did you have a calling for the priesthood?", Molly pried. "Yes, in a way I did. I always wanted to help people and the church was a big part of my growing up", he explained to her. Helena looked at Molly and smiled. "You two have a lot in common".

Gary came walking up. "It looks like the two of you are getting to know one another". Helena laughed. "Well, yes, Molly has asked her normal questions about Father Bill", Helena told him. "Oh, I am sorry Father. I can't do a thing about that", Gary said laughing a little. "It is okay. If you don't ask you don't know", Father Bill responded. Helena spoke up and said, "Let's get to my apartment. I can't wait for you guys to see it". Gary said, "Sounds great, but I need to be back at the base in the morning". Father Bill said, "That's not a problem. I will pick you up. What time?". Gary was thankful for the ride, "Would seven be too early?". "No, I will be at Helena's at 7 o'clock!", Father Bill responded. "Thank you so much. If I am going to be back here for a while, I will have to get me a car", Gary said.

A few days passed. Molly and Helena were having such a great time. Molly was happy that Gary had found out that he was to be at Westover for one year. Helena was thrilled. She started crying. "Don't cry", Molly told her, "I told you everything would work out just fine. The good thing is we can live on the base this time for the year. Then, who knows what will happen. Gary is going to check on the base housing today".

A couple days had passed, and Helena was going to have to go back to work at the deli. It was a beautiful late Spring day. Flowers were blooming. "Let's take a walk", Helena told Molly,

"I want you to meet Mr. Mack. He owns the bakery downstairs". "Ok, sounds good. I am in the mood for something sweet. Then we can walk it off", Molly replied. Molly laughed and Helena smiled. "You are so silly. You never change Molly. You make the world a better place".

As they walked in the bakery, Molly said, "This smells wonderful and makes me very hungry". They walked up to the counter and Mr. Mack walked out. "This must be your friend" he asked. "Yes, this is Molly Harper", Helena told him. "Nice to meet you Molly", he said. "Yes, nice to meet you", Molly responded. "Are you glad to be back at Westover? Helena told me your husband was in the Air Force", he asked. "Yes, we will be here for a year. I think I will even enjoy the winter and snow after being on Guam all that time. It was so hot and humid", she told him. "Enjoy this beautiful day", Mr. Mack told the girls. He handed Helena a bag full of pastries. "No money today. You young ladies just enjoy them". The girls thanked him and headed out the door. "He is very nice" Molly said. "Yes, he is. Don't know much about him. He is French", Helena told her. "Yes, I could tell that", Molly agreed.

Molly and Helena walked and talked. "We will be moving on the base at the end of the week. Our household things will be here about that time. And, Gary bought an old car from one of the guys in his squadron. So, I will be able to come see you anytime I want", Molly told Helena. "That is great Molly. I am so glad you are here. This year is going to be wonderful", Helena gushed. "It sure is Helena", Molly agreed.

A few months passed and everyone was settled in. Helena was going to mass every Sunday. She and Father Bill had become great friends. Molly and Gary spent a lot of time with Helena. Helena loved her job at the bakery. Her life had finally gotten back to normal.

Chapter Nine

It WAS A BEAUTIFUL SUMMER DAY. HELENA HAD WOKEN UP EARLY with the smell of the fresh bread baking. She knew she would have to stop in the bakery before she walked to work. Mr. Mack was always so nice to her. She got dressed and fixed her hair. She knew she was feeling happy again and that was good.

Helena opened the door to the bakery. It smelled so good. Mr. Mack was back behind the counter. He was busy talking so she waited for him to finish his conversation. All of a sudden, Helena got a strange feeling come over her. Mr. Mack came walking up to her. She could not believe her eyes. The person he is talking to is Andre. Their eyes met, but neither said a word.

Mr. Mack spoke up and said, "Hi Helena, this is my cousin, Andre from Paris". Helena could not speak. Andre walked up to her and gave her a hug. She almost fainted. "What are you doing here Helena?", he was surprised to see her too. "I live upstairs", she mustered up. "What are you doing back in Massachusetts?", Andre asked. Mr. Mack said, "Do you two know one another?". Helena said, "Yes, we do from a long time ago". Mr. Mack said, "My cousin will be working here for a while until he gets back on his feet. He has lived in Paris for some time". Helena could not take her eyes off of him. The love she was feeling for Andre didn't seem possible. She knew they were going to have to see each other and talk. Helena said, "I better get going to work. Thanks, Mr. Mack, for the pastries". Andre looked at her and smiled. He said, "Hope to see you again". "Oh, I am sure you will. I live upstairs in the back apartment", she told him. As she walked away there were a million things going through her head. Maybe he was married or has a girlfriend. I have to know. She knew from that moment she could not deny the love she still had for him. Her heart was pounding in her chest. She needed to get to work and take her mind off of him.

A couple days later it was Sunday. Helena was walking to mass thinking about Andre. She had not seen him since the day at the bakery. Maybe he didn't love her anymore, but she knew she would never stop loving him.

As she went in the church it had already filled up. So, she sat down in the back. She kneeled down to pray. She felt someone sit beside her. She moved over a little bit. When she finished praying, she opened her eyes and looked over. It was Andre. He smiled at her and reached over and put her hand in his. He held it so lovely. She smiled back. He looked at her and said, "I love you Helena. We need to talk". Helena just shook her head too agree but didn't respond.

When mass was over, they hurried out of the church. Helena told Andre to come with her, "We will go to my apartment and talk". He held her hand as they walked. Helena had so many questions. "What are you doing here? How come you came back?", she asked. "There was no reason for me to stay in Paris. My uncle really didn't need me anymore. I wanted to come home even though my parents are gone. I still have some family here. I never dreamed you would be here. I couldn't believe it when I saw you in Paris. How come you and your husband are here? Did the air force send you back?", he responded. "My husband is not here Andre. He was killed in a helicopter crash in Guam", Helena told him. "Oh, Helena, I am so sorry", Andre was not sure what else to say. "It is okay. It has been a while now. He was a wonderful man. He knew all about us Andre and he understood. He knew he wasn't my first love and he did everything possible to make me happy and he did. I knew I would never stop loving you", she told him. They reached the apartment. "Come in and let's talk about all of this".

Helena unlocked the door and they walked in. "This is very nice Helena", he complimented. "Thank you, it is perfect for me. Would you like a cup of coffee?", she asked. "Yes, that would be nice", he answered. "Have a seat. I will bring it out to us", she told him.

Helena was getting ready to pour the coffee in the cups and she looked up and there stood Andre. Their eyes met. He reached out and pulled her in to him. "I never stopped loving you Helena. I was only living for the day I could hold you in my arms. I didn't think it could ever happen, but I prayed every day that God would put you back in my life". "I love you too Andre. This is wonderful. It feels like a dream", Helena was overwhelmed with emotions. They kissed and cried and held each other for so long. "I want to make a life with you Helena and love you until we are old. I want to marry you", Andre proclaimed. "I want that too Andre. We should go talk to Father Bill. He knows all about our story and I need for you to meet Molly. If it wasn't for her I would have never survived these few years", Helena agreed. "Whatever you say Helena. I don't ever want to lose you again", Andre said to her.

After a few hours of talking, Andre said, "I better go. I have to work tomorrow for Mack. He is letting me stay at his house for a while". "I will let you know when I make an appointment with Father Bill", Helena responded. "Sounds good. Please know I love you so much", he told her. He kissed her on the cheek and went out the door.

Helena's emotions were going crazy. She was laughing and crying. She couldn't believe it. Andre loved her and wanted to marry her. This is happening so fast. Father Bill would help her. She knew she didn't want to go a minute longer without him, but was it too soon to want to marry him?

A few days later she was to see Father bill at 4 o'clock after she got off work. She hurried to the church. As she walked in, she saw Father Bill up at the alter lighting some candles. She waited for him to finish. Then she walked up. "Hello Helena. So good to see you. You sounded so excited when you called on the phone", he said. "Yes, Father, I have some exciting news", Helena was giddy with excitement to tell him. "Well, let's go to my office. That way you can speak openly", Father Bill pointed the way. She followed him. He told her to come in and have a seat and asked what was going on that was so exciting. "You are not going to believe this", she said. "Don't cry Helena, it is okay", he was confused he thought this was going to be good news. "Father, they are tears of joy. Andre is here in town. I couldn't believe my eyes when I saw him. He has come home, and he wants to marry me. And, I want to marry him. We never stopped loving one another", she told him all about how they ran into each other again. "When can I meet this young man?", Father Bill asked with a smile on his face. He was happy for Helena. "How about tomorrow afternoon about this same time? We can come to your office", Helena said. "That will work for me Helena", he told her. "Molly and Gary are going to meet him tonight. I just can't believe this is happening", Helena was happy, anyone who looked at her could tell. Father Bill hugged Helena and said to her, "See Helena, everything comes in the right time. You never stopped believing that God has a plan for you".

Helena was so nervous waiting for everyone to arrive. She paced the floor. What if Molly and Gary didn't like Andre? They know how my heart was broken, but it was not Andre's fault. His heart was broken too. It was his parents that caused all of this. But it has passed. This is a new chapter in my life and I so want Andre in it. There was a knock on the door. Helena's heart skipped a beat. She opened the door to see Andre holding flowers. "I want you to have these", he told her. "Thank you, please come in. Molly and Gary will be here soon", her heart skipped a beat again just seeing him.

Andre stood there looking at Helena. "What is it Andre?", she asked. "I am just looking at how beautiful you are", he walked up close to her, "Please Helena, may I hold you? I have dreamed of this day thinking it would never happen". "Oh, Andre, I love you so much", she replied. They embraced in one another's arms and Andre lifted her head up and kissed her. "Helena, I want to spend the rest of my life married to you. Please marry me. I know this seems sudden, but our love needs to be together", he told her. There was a knock on the door and Helena heard Molly saying, "Anybody home?". "Come on in", Helena yelled back. Helena and Andre stopped and backed away from one another.

Molly and Gary came through the door. "Molly, Gary, this is Andre", Helena told her friends proudly. "So nice to meet you", Andre said, and Gary shook his hand. "Andre, I have heard so much about you through the years. I feel like I know you", Molly gave him a hug. Andre looked at Helena, "Get used to it. She is a hugger and a talker. She can have you telling her your life story before you know what is going on". They all laughed. "Here, Helena, I brought some cookies. Let's make the coffee".

They talked for about an hour. Andre said, "You two know our story and we want to get married as soon as we can". "I agree", Molly said. She continued, "Your unforgettable love needs to get on with life. You two need each other. Where would you get married?". "I don't know. We want to ask Father Bill if he will marry us. I've never been married, and Helena is a widow so maybe we could be marred in the church", Andre responded. Molly said, "This is so exciting. I can't believe it is all happening. You two can finally have the life you were supposed to have".

The day had come to meet with Father Bill and ask him if he could marry them. Helena and Andre walked into Father Bill's office. "Hello, please come in and have a seat". Father Bill had such a smile on his face. Helena felt like he knew what they wanted.

Helena spoke up, "Father Bill, Andre and I want to get married and we wanted to know if you would marry us". Helena had tears in her eyes and Andre held her hand so tight. "Of course, I will be happy to marry you two", he was still beaming for them. Helena and Andre both started to cry. Father Bill said, "Stop that or I will start crying. When do we want to do this?". They both said soon. "Let's look at my calendar. What kind of ceremony do you want?", he asked them. "Something small. Molly and Gary will stand up with us. Just the four of us. We want it to be in the church", Helena explained. "I have a Saturday open two weeks away", he told them. "Great!", Helena said, "That is perfect. That will give us time to get our marriage license and Andre has a job interview next week. We will live in my apartment for a while until we get on our feet".

Helena and Andre hugged Father Bill and left holding hands. As they got to the bottom of the steps, Andre pulled Helena into him. He kissed her like she had never been kissed. "I love you Helena and I will take care of you and love you forever and until the end of time". Helena looked at Andre and said, "After that kiss two weeks seems like a long time". They both laughed. "Yes, it does", Andre said.

Helena was busy getting a dress. Molly was so excited to help her. It was just going to be a small ceremony. Then they would be married. Helena told Molly while they were shopping "We just want to finally be married". "What about a honeymoon Helena?", Molly asked. "We will drive up the coast. There is a cottage up there and Andre has made arrangements for us to spend a couple nights. I am so excited to spend the rest my life with him", Helena responded. "Well, it won't be long now", Molly replied smiling from ear to ear.

June 6th had finally rolled around; the wedding would happen. Helena told Andre that they would meet at the church. Molly said, "Come on Helena, get your dress on we need to go". As she stepped into the light lavender dress she couldn't stop smiling. "Oh, my Helena, you look beautiful. Here are your flowers, a plane white peace Lilly", Molly was in awe of her best friends' beauty. "Just perfect", Helena responded.

As they arrived at the church, Father Bill was standing at the door. He held his hand out to Helena. "You look beautiful. Come Andre is waiting he is so excited. I think Gary has had to calm him down a few times". Helena had decided to go straight to the alter where Andre was waiting. Father Bill was ready to marry them. Molly and Gary stood at the alter with them.

Father Bill said, "This makes me so happy to join you two in marriage". Father Bill blessed them and said his wedding prayers, and, in a few minutes, they were husband and wife. Helena almost fainted from joy and happiness. Father Bill hugged Helena and shook Andre's hand. "May you two love each other every day for the rest of your lives".

Molly was crying so hard she could not speak. She was happy for Helena. The unforgettable love she has for Andre has finally come back to her. "You deserve all that love and happiness Helena. Go to your cottage and spend time together", she told Helena through her happy tears. "Oh Molly, thank you so much for the love and friendship. I could have never made it this far without you. You told me once that everything happens for a reason and it's the right time. And that's when we trust God, he always takes care of us. He has brought Andre back into my life and now I am his wife and I know with the love we have for each other nothing can get in our way. This is the beginning of a wonderful life. I couldn't be any happier", she responded.

Andre walked up to Helena, took her hand in his and said, "Let's go my beautiful wife". They walked to the car. He opened the door and before she got in, he held her in his arms. "I love you Helena". He kissed her passionately. She kissed him back. "I love you Andre and will forever and always".

The End.

To order additional copies of

Unforgettable Love

visit Amazon at www.amazon.com
or
visit your local bookstore

www.ingramcontent.com/pod-product-compliance
Lightning Source LLC
Chambersburg PA
CBHW071416170626
46811CB00003B/1428